The Flying Tortoise

An Igbo Tale

Retold by Tololwa M. Mollel
Illustrated by Barbara Spurll

TORONTO OXFORD NEW YORK
OXFORD UNIVERSITY PRESS
1994

To Martin and Pat Msseemmaa
and Family
—T.M.M.

To Geoffrey Blackman Spurll,
1925–1988
—B.S.

Oxford University Press
70 Wynford Drive, Don Mills, Ontario, M3C 1J9

Toronto Oxford New York
Delhi Bombay Calcutta Madras Karachi
Kuala Lumpur Singapore Hong Kong Tokyo
Nairobi Dar es Salaam Cape Town
Melbourne Auckland Madrid

and associated companies in
Berlin Ibadan

Canadian Cataloguing in Publication Data

Mollel, Tololwa M. (Tololwa Marti)
The flying tortoise

ISBN 0-19-540990-6

1. Igbo (African people) — Legends. 2. Turtles — Folklore. 3. Legends — Africa. I. Spurll, Barbara. II. Title.

PS8576.055F5 1994 j398.24'52792 C93-093831-3
PZ8.1.M6F1 1994

Design: Kathryn Cole

1 2 3 4 — 7 6 5 4

Printed in Hong Kong

Long, long ago, Mbeku the tortoise had a magnificent shell. It was so smooth and clear and shiny, it even glowed in the dark. And because Mbeku was so handsome, he thought he deserved the lion's share of everything, especially food. Mbeku had a bottomless hole for a stomach and would stop at nothing to fill it.

One day in the forest, Mbeku found birds celebrating in a clearing. Curious, he asked what was happening.

"We just received a special invitation," cooed a dove. "The king of Skyland sent his messenger to ask us Earth-dwellers up for a feast."

"Well! I am an Earthdweller," Mbeku put in quickly. "I must come with you!"

"But you can't fly!" a swallow said, laughing.

Mbeku grinned slyly. "If you were to give me some feathers, I could."

Mbeku was known to be a troublemaker. Afraid he would spoil the fun, the birds all said no.

"Have it your way," warned Mbeku, "but you certainly need me. Skylanders are strange creatures. I know a lot about them, for I once had a friend from Skyland."

"You did?" gasped the foolish birds.

"Ah, the interesting things he taught me! If I went with you, I could be your spokesman and adviser."

The birds thought it over and realized they knew very little about the Skylanders and their customs. If Mbeku was telling the truth, he might be useful.

So each bird gave Mbeku some feathers. "We'll leave when you are ready," promised a parrot.

Mbeku took the feathers to Ngwele the lizard and asked her to help him make wings. Ngwele was a wonderful maker of things and was Mbeku's only friend.

Ngwele toiled all night while Mbeku perfected his plan. The next day, when the tortoise joined the birds, he was wearing a glorious pair of wings and a cunning smile.

"The Skylanders love fancy names," Mbeku told the birds. "They will think we are boring unless we choose the fanciest new names imaginable."

"What a fine idea!" agreed the vain birds. Soon they were dancing and singing out the new names they had chosen.

Finally, Mbeku announced, "My new name is . . ." He paused importantly. "Aaaaalllll-of-You!"

The birds burst out laughing. "Aaaaalllll-of-You! What kind of name is that?"

They were still laughing as they flew off to Skyland.

The king of the Skylanders welcomed the guests with a grand festival.

As spokesman, Mbeku introduced the birds by their fancy new names. But to their surprise, he majestically introduced himself as, "Aaaaallll-of-You—*king* of the Earthdwellers."

The Skylanders were very impressed. "How magnificent he is! Long live King Aaaaallll-of-You!"

They cheered and flapped their speckled wings, and their masks gleamed in the sunlight. Their stilt legs hammered the ground and their crimson robes swirled as they sang and danced and swayed.

Then, to the delight of the hungry birds, the Skylanders served a feast—bountiful heaps of mouthwatering fruits, berries, nuts, and honeycombs.

Mbeku bowed low. "A thousand thanks, noble king. But allow me to ask: for whom have you prepared this royal feast?"

The king spread his arms wide and spoke to the crowd in front of him. "Why, for aaalll of you, of course!"

Trickster Mbeku turned to the birds. "Skylanders always feed the spokesman first," he hissed. "So don't any of you touch the food. You heard the king name who this meal is for, and you know whose name that is!"

And with that, Mbeku dug into the feast.

Surprised, the Skylanders murmured to one another, "It must be the custom of the Earth-dwellers to let their king eat first."

"Don't worry," Mbeku mumbled to the birds. "Your turn will come."

But after Mbeku was finally done, there wasn't a scrap left for the birds, and it was time to depart.

A thick cloud descended as the king led the Earthdwellers to an enormous tree at the edge of Skyland. For a moment the fog parted and the birds saw their forest far, far below. The Skylanders bid their visitors goodbye, then disappeared back into the mist.

All at once, the angry birds set upon greedy Mbeku, ripped off his wings, and threw them over the edge of Skyland.

"No!" cried Mbeku, as his wings sailed out of sight. "How will I ever get back to Earth?"

"You should have thought of that before you spoiled our feast!" squawked a furious hornbill.

So, Mbeku put on a great show. He wept and wailed and claimed he was sorry. He promised this and he promised that, if only the birds would help him. One by one, they took pity on the pathetic creature before them.

"But what can we do?" asked the swallow. "Your wings are gone."

"Please," begged cunning Mbeku, "fly down to my friend Ngwele and ask her to build a huge pile of all the softest things she can find in the clearing. Do this for me and I will never trick you again."

The instant the birds had left, Mbeku's tears stopped. He grinned, then he laughed wildly. "Silly fools," he howled, holding his full, fat stomach, "to trust me yet again. How so clever I am! How so very clever! I've had their feast and now they'll help me get home!"

But unseen, the little swallow had hung back to hunt down a flea in her feathers. From the shadows she heard and saw everything. Quick as a wink, she was off and telling the others how, once more, they had been fooled.

This was too much. Greatly annoyed, the birds planned a trick of their own.

Ngwele was crafting a shelter for the coming rainy season when the birds found her.

"Mbeku has decided to stay longer in the sky," they said. "But he wanted us to ask you to gather all the *hardest* things you can find and build a huge pile in the clearing."

"What for?" asked Ngwele.

"He didn't say," replied a hummingbird. Then the birds disappeared deep into the forest to wait until the rains had come and gone.

From Skyland, Mbeku watched a tiny dot below. As Ngwele hurried back and forth, the pile she was building grew. To the tortoise it looked just like what he wanted. "Good," he muttered. "Now for a nice, soft landing."

He took aim and a deep breath. Then he jumped. Down, down he hurtled, the wind whistling in his ears.

W-o-o-o-o-o-o-o-o-o-o-o-o-o-o!
“I hope I took good aim!” Mbeku cried.

W-o-o-o-o-o-o-o-o-o-o-o-o-o-o!
“I hope the wind doesn’t blow me away!”

W-o-o-o-o-o-o-o-o-o-o-o-o-o-o!
“I hope the pile is soft enough!”
W-o-o-o-o-o-o-o!

He fell and fell and fell. And just when Mbeku began to wonder if he would ever land, he did!

The crash thundered through the forest.

Groaning beside the huge pile of rocks, bones, and tree stumps lay poor, badly bruised Mbeku, his shell scattered in a million pieces.

"Oh, your shell!" cried Ngwele, when she saw what had happened. "Your magnificent shell!"

Determined to put the shell back together, Ngwele began to collect the pieces. She had just gathered the last, tiniest bits when the rains came splashing down.

In the comfort of her shelter, all through the rainy season, Ngwele labored over the shell while Mbeku looked on.

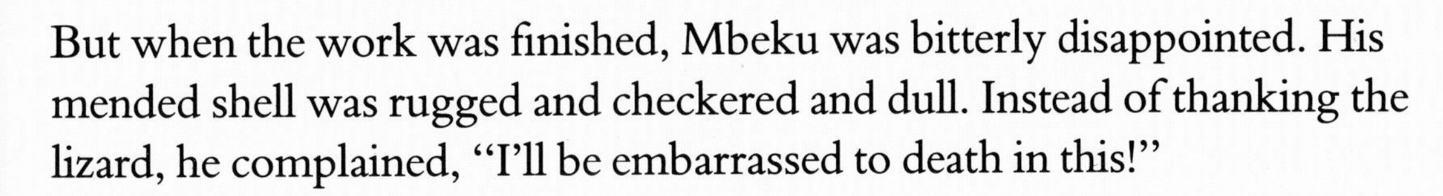

But when the work was finished, Mbeku was bitterly disappointed. His mended shell was rugged and checkered and dull. Instead of thanking the lizard, he complained, "I'll be embarrassed to death in this!"

"I did my best," sighed weary Ngwele. "No one could have done better. It's a miracle I managed to patch it up at all."

Early one morning, long after the rains had ended, Mbeku dared to take his first walk in the forest. He had not gone a dozen steps when he heard familiar twittering coming his way.

"Birds," muttered Mbeku. "The last creatures I want to meet in my hideous shell!"

Then Mbeku did something that has become his habit to this day. He drew himself into his checkered shell and lay as still as a stone.

Babbling merrily, the birds landed all around him. A pigeon and the swallow, thinking Mbeku was a rock, perched right on top of him.

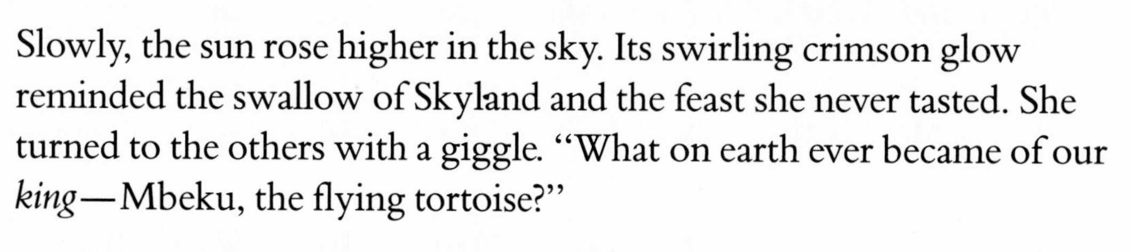

Slowly, the sun rose higher in the sky. Its swirling crimson glow reminded the swallow of Skyland and the feast she never tasted. She turned to the others with a giggle. "What on earth ever became of our *king*—Mbeku, the flying tortoise?"

"Who cares," remarked the hornbill. "He must be far from here bothering somebody else by now."

The birds all laughed to think they had finally outsmarted Mbeku, the trickiest of creatures. Their merriment increased until it rang and echoed through the trees.

That is why not one of them noticed when a certain rock began chuckling too.

END NOTE

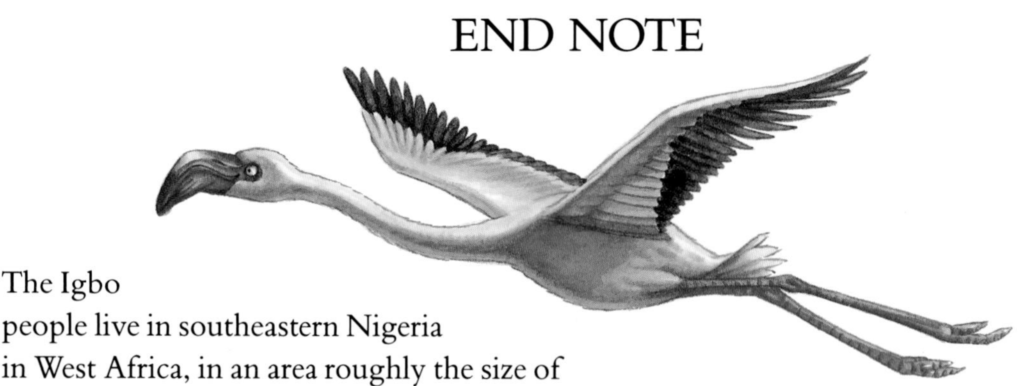

The Igbo people live in southeastern Nigeria in West Africa, in an area roughly the size of Switzerland. They have a strong oral culture and a large body of traditional children's stories kept alive by generations of storytellers. The tales are designed to teach children accepted norms and mores of society.

However, for the lessons to be successful and memorable, the stories must be entertaining —a fact that makes the tortoise Mbeku (m-bay-coo) a popular character. He is a lively, amusing trickster found in dozens of Igbo folktales. He is a mischief-maker always up to something, a schemer who makes things happen, for better or worse. *The Flying Tortoise*, in its various versions, is one of the most popular of the Igbo tortoise stories.

Time after time in many of the tales, Mbeku's gluttony, selfishness, cunning, and overconfidence land him in trouble and earn him ridicule. His plight is the obvious deterrent against unbecoming social conduct. But even as audiences laugh at the tortoise's foibles and excesses, they delight in the traits that make him the trickster he is. He is smart, funny, and resourceful, a true survivor who invariably finds his way into another story.

Tortoise stories among the Igbo are far more than lessons in good manners; they are a celebration of ingenuity and irrepressible spirit.